# MIND YOUR MANNERS

### by Michael Scotto
### illustrated by The Ink Circle

STaRRiNG

BUN O. BoBo
The BaKeR

BeaKeR O. BoBo
The SCiENTiST

Beaker the scientist worked every day in her lab. One Saturday, she heard a knock at the door.

"Posta, how are you today?" Beaker asked.

"I'm just fine," Posta replied. "I have a letter for you."

"For me?" Beaker asked. "I haven't gotten a letter in months!"

Beaker opened the letter and read it to Posta. "We are pleased to announce that you are the winner of the Midlandian Bobel Prize for Science!"

"**That's great, Beaker!**" Posta cried.

"Science is very important to any community," Beaker read. "To honor your study of the blueberry, we are holding a special banquet at the Town Square on Sunday night. There, you will receive your award."

"Congratulations!" Posta said. But Beaker's face became a frown. "What's wrong?" Posta asked.

"I can't go to the banquet," Beaker sighed. "I'm a whiz in the lab, but I never know how to act at fancy dinners. I just don't have good manners."

"You could practice," Posta suggested.

"But the banquet is on Sunday night," Beaker said. "That's tomorrow!"

"Then we'd better hurry!" Posta replied.

Beaker zoomed down the road in Posta's mail cart.

"Where are we going?"
Beaker asked.

"If you need to learn about manners," Posta answered, "there's only one place to practice." Beaker climbed out of Posta's cart in front of the bakery. "If anyone can help you," Posta said, "it's Bun."

Beaker sat at a table, and Bun swiftly
stepped up beside her. "Bonjour! Thank you for
choosing the Blueberry Bakery and Bistro. How
can I serve you?" Beaker explained her problem
to Bun. "It's probably not as bad as you think."
Bun said, "Let me set this table and get you a pie."

Today's
Special

Blueberry
Pie

In a flash, Bun set up a
perfect table for Beaker, with a
steaming blueberry pie. "Now,"
Bun said, "show me how you
would eat at a fancy dinner."

Beaker picked up the pie and plunged her face into it. "Wait, Beaker!" Bun cried.
"This is scrumptious!" Beaker said, her face purple. "Try it!"

"That's all right," Bun said. "Really!"

Beaker quickly calculated how far away Bun's mouth was, and she flicked him a big spoonful of pie. The pie flew across the room and landed right on Bun's nose.

"**Oops, sorry!**" Beaker said. "I guess my numbers were off."

Bun blew the berries out of his nose, only to see Beaker making a mountain out of her blueberry filling. "Beaker, you can't make a mountain out of your food!" Bun said.

"It's not a mountain," Beaker said, through a mouthful of pie. **"It's a volcano!"**

Beaker's blueberry volcano **exploded** and pelted the entire shop. Bun's other customers shrieked and ran as their clothes were stained **blue** and **purple**.

"That is enough!"
Bun cried. "If we practice
any longer, I won't have
any of my shop left."

"**You see?**" Beaker moaned. "I should just say that I can't come to accept my award."

"**Wait,**" Bun said. "I'm sorry for losing my temper. Let's start again."

"That would be great," Beaker said, as she wiped her face clean with the tablecloth.

Bun snatched the tablecloth away. "**First!**" he exclaimed. "Never wipe your mouth or face with the tablecloth."

"What should I use?" Beaker asked.

Bun showed her a napkin. "Always use a napkin to keep yourself clean."

"**Oh!**" Beaker said. "I thought that was just a decoration!"

Bun held up a knife and fork. "There are some special foods that you can eat with your hands," Bun said, "but most times, you need to use your knife and fork. If you aren't sure, use a knife and fork just to be safe. They will help you to cut your food into bite-sized pieces. **Watch how I do it.**"

Bun quickly set a fresh table to demonstrate. "It is nice that you wanted to share with me," Bun said as he carefully cut a bite. "But you should never, ever throw food. **That is not good manners.**"

"Is there anything else I should know?" Beaker asked.

"Yes," Bun said. "I know that you're a scientist, but the dinner table is no place for doing experiments. You should not play with your food."

"I understand," Beaker said with a nod. "I sure made a mess, didn't I? **Let me help you clean up.**"

After Beaker helped Bun clean, she went home to rest for her big dinner the next night.

The next day, she picked out her best dress and went to the banquet.

Beaker shared a table with Posta. "Did Bun help you?" Posta asked.

"He sure did," Beaker replied. "You really know how to deliver."

"Here comes dinner!" Posta said.

Beaker carefully placed her napkin on her lap. "My, this blueberry roast looks wonderful!" She used her fork to taste it.

"What was the experiment that your award is for?" Posta asked. "Could you give me a demonstration?"

"I would," Beaker said, "but the dinner table is no place to play around. I can show you at my lab the next time you come by."

The rest of dinner went without a hitch, and soon it was time for Beaker to accept her award. "The most important part of my job is being ready to learn," Beaker said. "So, I would like to thank Bun, because without his teachings, I wouldn't be here tonight."

Everyone at the banquet burst into applause, including Bun, who happily watched his newest student return to her table and finish her meal with excellent manners.

# DISCUSSION QUESTIONS

Why is it important to use good manners?

Can you think of examples of using good manners that are not mentioned in the story?